ANUNG'S JOURNEY

Based on an ancient Ojibway legend
as told by Steve Fobister

CARL NORDGREN

Illustrations by Brita Wolf

Torchflame Books

To Marie and her love.
To Steve Fobister and his magic.

OTHER BOOKS BY CARL NORDGREN

The *River of Lakes* Series:
The 53rd Parallel
Worlds Between

PROLOGUE

My hands were freezing from digging in the snow. But I could not stop. I was too embarrassed to give up. I would not admit I had been so wrong.

I was just ten years old.

The day before, on Christmas Eve morn, I snowshoed back into the forest to chop down a small spruce sapling to be our Christmas tree. I built a base for it with some stones and it stood next to the cabin where I lived during the winters with my grandfather and my grandmother. The cabin was on the English River, on the Grassy Narrows Reserve in northwestern Ontario.

It snowed heavily on Christmas Eve. Overnight there were another couple of feet of white powder on top of a foot of settled snow from the weeks before. When I looked out the window on Christmas morning I saw the tree was half buried by the great drift at its base.

Hidden under all that snow around the base of the tree, I knew there was a great pile of Christmas presents for me and the other children of Grassy Narrows. So I pulled my boots on and slipped into my coat as I dashed outdoors. My grandmother called to me to take my gloves but I did not return for them.

I was eager to see the presents Santa Claus brought. Ah gee, I can still remember how excited I was as I dug and I dug in the snow, calling out to the nearby cabins, promising presents for everyone, even as my hands began to burn with cold.

I am Steve Fobister. I am Anishinaabe. The French who settled in Canada called us Ojibway. The English called us Chippewa.

I was once Chief of the First Nations Grassy Narrows Ojibway.

I was born in a wigwam on the banks of the English River, where the river opens into many lakes. When I was born my family's village was on the shore of Kee Ta chee won. That means "the lake where the shores burned with fires of great mourning."

Until I was 13 my family traveled the river's chain of lakes in a family clan that once grew so large it filled five big freight canoes with uncles and aunts and cousins and all who were members of the Loon clan. We only lived on the Reserve in the winter in those days.

My people call those days the frontier times. In the frontier times my grandfather and my uncles hunted moose and deer with their rifles and taught me and my cousins how to hunt with rifles too, for they were most effective, and we hunted to feed ourselves.

But first they showed us how to make bows and arrows and how to hunt the old ways.

When I was still a young boy they taught us to hunt partridge and ducks with a sling. And to catch rabbits in a snare. We learned to make our contributions early to the meat we ate.

They also taught us how to fish with gillnets, for walleye and lake trout. And to fish at night with the light of a torch to attract bugs that would attract small fish so we could spear the big pike when they would come close to feed on the bait fish.

We worked the trap lines with our fathers and uncles and grandfathers to learn to trap muskrat and beaver—and mink and fisher and fox. To preserve the meat and fish for a long cold winter the women smoked some of it. And they dried some of it.

With the youngest children helping, the women also collected blackberries, gooseberries, and we were rich with blueberries in those frontier days.

Everyone harvested manoomin in August and September. That is what you call wild rice. We call the times of the manoomin harvest Manoominike-Giizi. That means the Manoomin Moon.

My cousins and I worked with the men and the women every day. We learned from watching them, then while helping them. We learned how to build shelters. The Nokomis taught us where to find the herbs that restore health, how to prepare them, what to say as you apply them so you call on their full healing powers.

We learned to birth babies by watching our midwives. And we heard what they said, and what the elders said, to call the spirits to protect a new life, and to thank the Great Creator for that new life.

We learned how to live in these forests as our grandfathers taught our fathers, as our grandmothers taught our mothers. When we were taught the old ways we were told it had always been this way. As I grew up I met many who lived their lives on the Reserve in all the seasons, and I believed it was my clan's good fortune to live the old ways on the river. I thanked

Grandfather for staying true to the ancestors.

Sometimes we would sleep in the heavy canvas miner tents we pitched on a quiet bit of shore but in the frontier times we still built birch-bark wigwams to sleep in. We camped one place early in the season. We moved to a new spot as the season's patterns of abundance shifted. Or when it was Manoominike-Giizi.

We would dress in traditional clothes when other family clans gathered together for pow-wows or tribal councils or for clan celebrations. Otherwise we dressed in clothes we traded furs for at the Hudson Bay Post.

We left the Reserve to travel the river as soon as the ice melted at the time we call Iskigamizige-Giizi, the Maple Sap Boiling Moon. We made our way living on the river until Gashkadino-Giizi, the Freezing Moon, forced us back to our winter camp at Grassy Narrows Reserve. The wood burning stoves in the cabins kept them warm even on the nights the temperature was -20.

In those frontier times we had no electricity. Just oil lamps.

The Reserve has been moved closer to Kenora now and today it has electricity but in the frontier times it was even further out in the wilderness, and even in the winters we lived on the Reserve, my grandfather tended to his trap lines and hunted, unless the worst winter storms and the coldest weather kept him in. Then we ate the food we'd helped the women preserve in the fall.

The winter before the big drift of snow covered the Christmas tree, the winter I was nine, that was the first winter we lived in a cabin on the Reserve. When we settled in I found an Eaton's mail order catalog lying in the corner of the cabin we were given.

I discovered Santa Claus in the catalog's pictures. When I asked my grandfather and grandmother who this man was in these pictures they said they did not know him. But our people have told many stories using simple pictographs and so I studied the pictures of him in the catalog, the different scenes of him in his workshop surrounded by tiny magical spirits and in his sleigh being pulled by flying caribou and then mysteriously sneaking into the houses of the white man at night to leave presents for everyone in the house under their tree.

I found a story in those pictures. This story told me that if I decorated a fir tree at Christmas this big bearded white man and his spirit helpers will make toys for me to play with, and put them in colorful boxes, and place them under the tree for me and all of the boys and girls of Grassy Narrows.

This white man and his sleigh filled with presents and pulled by flying caribou somehow was part of the white man's celebration of the birth of the baby Jesus, for there were pictures of the Christ child in the manager as well.

I went out into the forest and found a young fir that looked like the one in the pictures. The first year I brought the tree into the cabin and set it up there. I didn't have anything to put on the first tree that looked like the bright lights and colorful balls in the pictures. It filled much of the open space of the cabin, but it was a pretty tree.

Before I went to bed on Christmas Eve we stood around it and sang the songs about the baby Jesus the Jesuit's had translated into our language. Before I knew what the words meant I liked the soft peaceful sound of Christmas music. Sometimes I hummed Christmas melodies when I was walking a trap line or fishing for walleye.

When we finished our songs I climbed the ladder to the loft where my bed of furs and blankets waited for me.

I was excited about what the bearded white spirit would bring. That night I dreamed there were many presents under our tree for me and my grandparents and the other children.

When I awoke Christmas morning my grandparents were already awake, for we show the Great Creator how happy we are to spend another day in His Creation by rising to welcome the sun. In the winter, this far north, that is not too hard as the sun rises much later.

Our people call the Great Creator Gitche Manitou.

I wondered if my grandparents had seen the presents under the tree but I saw no sign of it on their faces. I was halfway down the ladder when I saw the floor under the tree was bare.

I was very sad for much of the day. My grandparents must have left me alone with my disappointment, for I can not remember anything they said or did. But before that day ended, I decided that I would do two things differently for next Christmas Eve.

I would figure out how to decorate the tree with colorful shapes, for all the pictures of the trees in the catalog were covered with decorations. And I would place the tree outside. This great bearded white spirit must not have seen it inside our cabin.

On our next trip to sell furs at the Hudson Bay Post I began collecting every colorful piece of paper I could find. When I traveled there with my uncle he would get me a candy bar and I carefully opened the wrapping so I could save it. I even retrieved candy wrappers and other colorful bits and pieces of paper from the dust bin.

By the time Christmas Eve came again and I chopped down a larger and even prettier spruce, I had a box filled with bright ornaments for my tree. I had folded some papers into animals. Some were stars. Some were flowers. I tied or stuck them all over my tree.

I remember that the people who lived in the closest cabins came to watch me prepare the tree. We sang Christmas songs and my friends and my cousins wondered what sort of presents we might get.

On Christmas morning I was climbing down from the ladder from my loft when my grandfather told me of the great snow during the night. I pulled back the blanket from the window and saw the tree was half covered in snow. I knew that high drift of snow hid a great collection of presents that the Santa Claus spirit had left. I ran out and began to dig furiously.

I imagined the toys were at the base of the fir where a small mound of stones held the tree in place. I had to dig through two or three feet of snow to get to it.

First my fingers burned from the cold. Then they grew numb. When I hit the stone base with nearly deadened fingers they barely felt anything but there was pain growing in my heart. By then I was already afraid there were no presents.

I pushed the tree with my shoulder to expose the ground behind it. There were no presents.

I kicked over the last mounds of snow. There were no presents.

Now I was not only very cold, I saw I was very foolish. As I was digging I saw my grandmother was watching me from the window. When I saw her I felt as if all our people were watching. I felt everyone knew I was a foolish little boy whose cries of delight were now filled with disappointment.

I ran back to the cabin to grab the ax. I found my gloves where I left them near the stove. I did not look at my grandfather or grandmother. If they said anything, I did not hear it. I went back outside with the ax.

I tried to chop the tree into pieces. First I was just swinging at it with the ax because my hands were still stiff and so numb I could not hold the handle properly. When my hands warmed up and I gained control of the ax, the tree quickly became a pile of pieces that I covered up in the snow.

I returned to the cabin, crying. My grandfather was sitting on a stool repairing a snowshoe. My grandmother was sitting on the floor at his feet, mending a blanket. My grandfather told me to sit down next to my grandmother, close to the stove. She draped the blanket over my shoulders.

My grandfather told me that he did not understand this white man spirit. He had never heard stories of his powers or his purpose. Then he reminded me that the white man has not been given all the gifts Gitche Manitou has given to our people. He said maybe it is a good thing that this spirit is sent to the white man to give some gifts to their children but we did not need these gifts for we have been given so much from the Great Creator.

Then he said it was time for me to hear one of the oldest stories of our people, one he was told by his grandfather when he was a boy. It was a story about a boy who was given many gifts from Gitche Manitou. He told me to listen carefully so I could tell it to my grandchildren.

There are many stories our people can only tell in the deepest of winter, the season we call Biboon. Many of the stories about animals and their spirits can only be told when the earth is frozen hard beneath a thick blanket of snow. This is one of those stories.

This story he told me that Christmas morning I have told so many winter nights to my children and to my grandchildren. And to my nieces and nephews who I have raised as my children.

Maybe the story has changed in some places over the years.

Yes, I am sure this is so.

But when I tell it I can still hear my grandfather telling it to me for the first time that Christmas morning so long ago.

THE STORY OF BLUE SKY

IN AN ANISHINAABE VILLAGE, there lived an orphan boy. This poor child's father died before he was even born, and then his mother passed from this world for the next soon after his birth.

The first name given to this baby boy by the women of his village was Blue Sky. The villagers agreed to call him Blue Sky to show the Great Creator that everyone living in this village will care for this orphan child. He was called Blue Sky by the women as their promise he would know the happiness a blue sky brings all the days of his life. The men called him Blue Sky as their promise they would teach him everything a man needs to know where ever he is found.

They called him Blue Sky to show the Great Creator that each one of the women of the village and each one of the men of this village would care for Blue Sky as if he was their own child each and every day.

This orphan boy lived long, long ago. It was before our ancestors first arrived in this place where our people have lived now for many generations. Blue Sky lived in the lands of our oldest ancestors to the East, in the days when our people were following the prophecy of the Great Megis.

This was so long ago the white man had not come and disturbed our life on Turtle Island.

The village where Blue Sky was born was very small. And the women who named him with their love bestowed it on him every day. Blue Sky would sleep next to the fire in one family's wigwam for many nights. Then another family would invite him to share their wigwam and food and fire.

As he grew from a baby to a child he heard all of the stories told at all of the night fires.

As he grew to be a boy the men of the village taught him what a man must know. The men took him to the bay when they fished with torches blazing at night and stood in the shallows and speared the pike that came too close.

One of the men taught him how to use a sling to hunt small game. He showed Blue Sky the small rapids where the smooth round stones were found that made the most accurate shot.

Another man taught him how to make a bow and arrows and how to shoot straight and true.

Another man gave Blue Sky the drum his father had played at the clan fires and told him to listen to the sounds about him and Blue Sky tried to play them on his drum.

Because Blue Sky was an orphan he learned each skill and craft from the man in the village who knew it best. He grew to be a skillful hunter. When he went out fishing he always brought home a pike or a walleye.

There were nights where Blue Sky felt very lonely. When he heard a mother singing her songs gently to a crying baby, on those nights he wished he knew his mother. On those nights he wished he had his own father. On those nights he might leave his bed by the night fire and search for a place to be alone. He would take his father's drum with him and play it softly so only his mother and father's spirits could hear it.

Most of the time Blue Sky was happy. When he was happy he would practice playing his drum to the beat of the young men's dances and he learned the songs of praise to Gitche Manitou.

The time passed and Blue Sky grew older. He was ready to leave childhood behind. It was time for him to go to the tall mountain his village held sacred. This was where the boys of his village would fast and pray to Gitche Manitou. This was the place they would pray for the dream vision that would show them how they must live their lives as men.

It was time for Blue Sky to pray for his vision but like many of the young boys he was afraid. He was afraid to be alone on the top of the mountain. He was afraid no dream would come to show him his life's purpose. He did not tell the people of the village of his fears. He tried to hide them. But when he was alone by the bank of the river he would beat his father's drum and the sound would drive his fears away.

The night before Blue Sky would leave for the mountain top all of the people gathered at the village fire circle. Some of the men remembered the nights they spent alone in the sacred place, waiting for their vision to find them, searching for signs that would lead them to understand their vision. They told Blue Sky the stories of what their visions meant to their lives.

As the night went on the Nokomis sang a song about Blue Sky's mother and father. The children who had earlier danced around the fire now lay quietly at the sides of their mothers and fathers.

Blue Sky sat alone.

The next day the men of the village led Blue Sky to the tall mountain ridge that looked out upon the spirit Waubun, the spirit of the East and the new day sun. The place they led him to was the highest peak in all the Four Directions.

The men could see Blue Sky was afraid. But it was time and they could see he was ready. They left him there alone.

Blue Sky fasted the first day, eating only the handful of blueberries that grew on the bushes near the peak.

He was afraid of sitting alone on the mountaintop, but he knew this was his time.

He was afraid, so he prayed to Gitche Manitou as the new sun rose on the second day.

And he prayed to Gitche Manitou as the wind rushed by.

He prayed to the spirit of Maang the Loon when the wind brought a loon's cry from the distant lake as the sun settled for its rest.

He prayed to the spirit of Gookooko'oo the Owl when its call echoed across the valley in the night.

But still Blue Sky was afraid. He was first afraid to be all alone. Then he grew fearful there was someone, or maybe something, back there in the forests, watching him. Once he was sure he heard something but when he turned there was nothing to see.

On the third day when Migizi the Eagle circled overhead and called out to the world the boy prayed to the spirits of all of the animals in the forests that heard the eagle's cry. And then he thanked Gitche Manitou for all of the gifts he had been given.

He was watching the sunrise on the fourth day when his vision came to him. In the bright morning sun light he saw how favored he had been to have all the men and all the women of this village care for him as if he were their first son. For in his vision he was standing before the greatest chief of all the First Nations people and he was telling this chief how the people of his village honored Gitche Manitou. He was standing in front of the greatest chief to tell him that his fathers and his mothers cared for him every day to give thanks to the Great Creator.

In his vision he could not see this greatest chief, for he was covered by a great mountain of snow white clouds that shined brightly. Just as the clouds were parting and Blue Sky would see the greatest chief, he was startled by a sound behind him, just outside the cleared mountain peak, and he turned to see what it was. There was nothing there, just a branch moving back into its place, and now his vision had left him.

But the meaning was clear to him. Blue Sky must find the greatest chief of all the people and tell him the story of his mothers and fathers of the village and of the many acts of kindness they have given to him.

This would be how he would begin his life as a man. Not to find the greatest chief of the Anishinaabe. Not the greatest chief of the Odawa or the Pottawattamie, the closest brothers of the Anishinaabe, who with us are the people of the Three Fires. His vision was to find the greatest chief of all the tribes of the First Nations. And in his vision the spirits were inviting him to begin his journey.

When the people of his village learned of the vision that came to Blue Sky they were proud of him. For every man of the village thought Blue Sky was his son. Every woman was his mother. They knew Gitche Manitou had chosen their son for a special journey.

Because Blue Sky was a son to everyone, the people of the village were sad for him to leave. There was such danger traveling so far alone in the forest for a young man who just the day before had been a boy. He could lose his way. He might get hurt climbing a mountain ridge or he might starve if he could not feed himself on such a long journey. And there were many evil spirits who live in the deepest parts of the forest.

The worst of these evil spirits was Windigo, the terrible one. Windigo, the cannibal.

That night the people of Blue Sky's village had a great feast in his honor. They celebrated his vision. In their songs they asked Gitche Manitou to watch over him like a first son. To protect him and to feed him. To lead him to sweet water and to dry shelter. And to keep him safe from Windigo.

The people sang deep into the night.

They asked Blue Sky to play his father's drum and sing his song of his vision. Blue Sky beat the drum while the people of his village danced. They danced until even the young men grew tired.

That night the people gave many gifts to Blue Sky to help him on his journey.

They presented these gifts in a beautiful pouch. Each of his mothers had sewn their most precious beads and shells in the design that decorated the pouch.

The pouch was filled with many things he would need on his journey.

THE VILLAGE CHIEF TELLS THE OLDEST STORY

BLUE SKY SPENT HIS LAST NIGHT in his village in the wigwam of the village chief. The chief told him many stories that night. He told him all the stories he had ever heard about the great chiefs for one of them might be the greatest chief of all the First Nations. All of the stories he knew told that the great chiefs lived far away in the lands where their ancestors lived before the Great Megis prophecy led them from their ancestral home. Blue Sky must journey far to the East, Waabinong, to the land of the first sun.

That night the chief told Blue Sky the oldest story. The first story. The story about Gitche Manitou and his dream.

Our people have always known this to be the first story for it is the only story that came from the time before the earth was first formed. That was when Gitche Manitou had his dream vision.

Gitche Manitou dreamed about a vast sky filled with stars.

Among the countless stars there was only one that was a radiant sun, and it bathed his dream with light.

In his dream there was a wonderful moon, magically filling his dream with mystery.

But it was the earth that was Gitche Manitou's favorite part of the dream.

On the earth he found great mountains shining golden under the bright sun, and he discovered green forests that covered the valleys.

The clear waters flowing through rivers and streams past quiet meadows into brilliant blue lakes delighted the Great Creator. That these lakes were filled with every sort of fish, and that the green forests were filled with every sort of animal, all of this was a wonder.

In Gitche Manitou's dream a giant eagle from the mountains flew down over the trees and landed in the top branches. A feather fell from the eagle and slowly drifted down where it landed at the feet of the most extraordinary animal of all.

These were the first people.

The Great Creator's dream showed life struggling to be born, and life ending, but never ending. For his dream showed life on earth is reborn again and again and that it will always be this way.

In his wisdom Gitche Manitou knew such a beautiful dream must be fulfilled. So out of nothing he made the universe of the sun, the moon, the stars that blanket the heavens, and the earth and all the life on it. And when he made man he made him out of material he hadn't used for any of his other creations.

When the village chief finished his story it was time for him to give Blue Sky his new name. He named him Anung, Morning Star. He told him how he must use the stars to guide his journey East and that is why he named him Anung.

The chief told Anung to direct his travel each day to the lands of the morning star, the sun. He showed Anung that the design sewn into his pouch included an image of the sun rising in the East, to remind Anung of his true path.

He told Anung to listen to the wind in the trees. To the animals' calls and cries. To his heart's whisper.

He told Anung that these are the ways Gitche Manitou will talk to him during his journey.

Then he told Anung about Windigo.

"Windigo lives in the deepest darkest places in the forest. He lives there all alone. That is why our people travel by water when moving from one place to another. Windigo does not like the water. But when you must travel through the forest he will follow behind you, waiting for the moment when you are not aware. He is as tall as a tree and white as the snow. His face has no nose and his mouth is filled with fangs. If he catches you, he will eat you."

The chief told Anung to listen for rustling in the leaves behind him. And to look for bloody footprints, for Windigo runs so fast his feet are always bleeding.

After Anung asked more questions about Windigo they grew quiet and stared at the fire for a long time. Anung was afraid about his long journey to find the greatest chief, but he knew this was his destiny. After a while they grew sleepy and settled to sleep at the side of the chief's fire.

THE JOURNEY BEGINS

ANUNG LEFT HIS VILLAGE early the next morning. He followed the path that headed East. All the people of his village watched him enter the forest. Each of his mothers cried her sorrow and each of his fathers called out his last advice.

He carried his pouch with food and the gifts the people had given him. Inside the pouch was his sling. Tied to his back were his snowshoes, as he was prepared for a long voyage that could take him through the winter. Over one shoulder was his father's drum and over his other shoulder was his bow and a quiver of the finest arrows each father crafted for him.

All morning he could stay true to his course by following this path through the forests that blanketed the first low ridges.

These forests were familiar to him, for his people traveled this path many times.

When the sun reached its peak the path came to a small river and followed along its bank to the South, Zwaawanong.

Anung drank some water and filled his water bottle, and rested.

If he stayed on the path he had been following he would not be heading East towards the place where he hoped to find the greatest chief of his people. If he stayed to his true direction he would be walking deep into the forests where he'd never traveled before and that made him so afraid.

As he sat there wondering what he should do, a voice spoke to him. Anung jumped to his feet in surprise and looked all around.

He saw no one about.

When the voice spoke again it called his name. "Anung, your journey takes you away from the paths of your village." That is when Anung saw that it was Turtle sitting on a log at the riverbank speaking these words to him.

"Hello Turtle. How do you know I am on a journey?"

"A young man who is still a boy would only travel so far from his village all alone if he was on a journey."

Anung told Turtle of his vision, and that his journey had just begun.

"I will go with you," said Turtle, "for I too would like to see the greatest chief of all the people. My great ancestor Mishee Mackinakong carries all the people of the First Nations on his back. I must see how the greatest chief of all the people honors Mishee Mackinakong."

When Turtle asked to come along on Anung's quest, Anung picked up Turtle and put him in his pouch. They crossed the river and walked into the dark forest where there was no path to guide their way.

Anung was afraid of the dark forest but he hid his fear by telling Turtle stories about his village and his mothers and his fathers. As they journeyed on, soon he forgot he was afraid.

TURTLE TELLS HIS STORY

THE DAY WAS LONG and they traveled a great distance.

It was late in the summer and the great spirit of Waabanɔng covered the bushes with blueberries. This is what they ate as they walked on.

As the sun set behind them they stopped. Anung made a shelter and a fire near the base of a great rock. On the rock face there were many pictures painted by his people and their ancestors. One picture showed there was a large river ahead. There were pictures that told him he would be entering the land of his brothers the Odawa in a day or two. Anung beat the drum as he looked at the pictures and as the drum beat filled the night the image of Deer began to leap and the image of Wolf began to run and the pictures of Bear and of his ancestors began to dance.

As they were lying down to sleep by the fire Anung asked Turtle to tell him the story about his ancestor carrying the greatest chief and all the people on his back. So Turtle told him his ancestor's story.

"Long ago great clouds covered the sky and rained down day after day until the entire earth was flooded. Even the tallest ridges were covered by the flood waters. When the water rose so high all of the original people Gitche Manitou created were drowned. All of the animals who lived on land died. Only the animals who could live in water survived this great flood.

"After much time passed the Mishee Mackinakong rose to the water's surface, for he could see that Sky Woman was lonely. The Great Turtle invited Sky Woman to come down and to rebuild the earth on the back of his massive shell.

"Sky Woman was very lonely and it brought her joy to accept Mishee Mackinakong's invitation. She gathered all the animals who had survived and asked them to fetch her some mud from the bottom of the deep waters for this is what she needed to rebuild earth.

"All the animals wanted to help Sky Woman. First Otter dove deep into the depths of the waters. Otter was underwater for a long time but when he surfaced he was out of breath and empty-handed.

"Then Beaver took his turn. He plunged into the water and swam deeper than ever before but he could not find the bottom and he finally had to return to the surface, exhausted from his try.

"Then Loon tried. She swam deeper and deeper and she stayed under for a long time but she failed to find the bottom for it was too dark and cold for her and she had to return.

"When Muskrat offered to retrieve the mud so Sky Woman could rebuild the earth all the other animals laughed at him. They did not think the small Muskrat was so strong or as important as they were.

"Muskrat did not let that bother him. He dove into the waters and he swam deep down into the cold and dark. He was down a long time. After a while the animals stopped laughing and were afraid for Muskrat for he had been underwater longer than any of them had. He was under the water a very long time.

"They had just given up hope that he could survive for so long underwater when his body rose to the surface and floated there, still as death. All the animals gathered round as Sky Woman breathed life into him and when Muskrat recovered it was discovered he was holding a small bit of mud in his paws. Sky Woman used this mud to rebuild the earth on the back of my ancestor's shell. To show her thanks, Sky Woman gave all the turtles the gift of understanding the languages of all of Gitche Manitou's creatures.

"That is why the people call this land Turtle Island. And that is why your people honor Muskrat."

ANUNG MEETS FISHER AND TROUT

THE NEXT MORNING as the sun rose Anung and Turtle were ready to travel. They walked many miles, resting and telling stories and gathering foodstuffs along the way. They could see the forest was opening ahead of them. They crossed a small ridge and looked down upon two lakes connected by a small river channel.

When they came close to the water they saw Fisher. They watched him run to the shore of the first lake and then pace back and forth, back and forth.

Fisher stopped when he spotted Northern Pike, swimming in the water in the weeds, close to shore.

"Hey you there Northern Pike. Do you know what Walleye is saying about you over there in the next lake? Oh, my, he says Northern Pike is a slimy thing. He says that you have a long ugly nose. Walleye says all the other fish laugh at your long nose and think you are the ugliest fish in all the rivers and lakes."

Then Fisher ran to the second lake where he found Walleye swimming near the rocky shore.

"Hey there. I was talking to Northern Pike in the next lake. He says Walleye has fat bulging eyes. He says all the other fish think your fat bulging eyes make you the ugliest fish in all the rivers and all the lakes. He says even Walleye think you are ugly and that is why you spend so much time in the deep dark waters."

Anung and Turtle watched Fisher run from one lake to the next one, telling more lies to Walleye and then telling more lies to Northern Pike. The fish were each getting angrier and angrier. Both of them swam in hard small circles they were so angry.

Fisher told Walleye that Northern Pike wanted to fight him. That Northern Pike was waiting for him in the middle of the channel that connected the two lakes. Then he told Northern Pike that Walleye was waiting there to fight him.

The fish swam to the middle of the channel and as soon as they saw each other they attacked and began to fight. They slashed and bit at each other with their sharp teeth. They were very angry and they fought a long time, biting each other over and over. Soon there was so much blood in the water they were fighting in a red swirling cloud of blood.

Each fish had badly wounded the other but they still fought on and on until they were both so weak they floated to the water's surface and that was when Fisher hopped down from the rock and jumped into the water and caught the two fish. Each fish was as big as Fisher but they were so weak now he could easily carry them to shore.

Fisher had never seen so much food at one time. He ate and he ate. Each fish was much bigger than any chipmunk or mouse he had ever caught.

Fisher kept eating and eating even as he grew fatter and fatter.

Marten came out from behind the tree. When he saw how fat Fisher had become and how much fish was left he asked Fisher to share it with him but Fisher said no and kept on eating. Marten waited a moment but when Fisher kept on eating he asked again if he would share the remaining fish. Fisher was much bigger than Marten and turned from his catch and tried to drive him away. But because he was so fat he was now very slow. Anung and Turtle watched as Marten showed he was too quick for the fat and sluggish Fisher. He darted around him again and again and was able to steal away all the fish he wanted.

For many days Anung and Turtle traveled deep into the forests. One day when Anung was stalking a grouse to shoot with his sling he heard something behind him but when he turned there was nothing there, just a branch moving as if the wind had been blowing.

But there was no wind. Whatever it was frightened the grouse and it flew safely away.

Every night he found a good place to build his fire and on many nights Turtle would tell him more stories. The night after he heard something following him Anung was lonely for his village and afraid of the night spirits that haunted the deepest forests and he beat his father's drum to remember the songs his mothers and fathers had taught him. Most nights he was still excited from the day's journey exploring new lands and he would beat the drum and sing a song of the many new things he had seen. But this night he played his drum to sing the songs that called on the spirits to protect him.

Each morning he and Turtle headed off towards the land of the first sun. Now there were many kinds of nuts though fewer berries along the way. The forests were filled with grouse and when he used his sling to kill one of them, it fed him for two days.

Each night when he settled into his campsite he set snares to catch rabbits.

When his camp was near a river or lake, he made fish traps to catch walleye or perch.

The men of his village had taught him well. And Gitche Manitou was watching over him. So he was not hungry. He was warm at night. But he was never relaxed for now it seemed that nearly every day he heard or felt something back there, back in the forest, following him. Turtle didn't hear anything, and tried to assure Anung, but Anung had learned that a turtle doesn't hear very well.

After many days traveling through the forests Anung saw signs that people lived nearby.

He came upon a path that led him through the spruce trees then out of the forest into a field of corn, a field much bigger than any Anung's village had grown. On the far side of the corn field Anung could see the edge of a village that was much larger than his.

Anung had never seen so many corn plants growing in one place before. So many plants meant there were many mouths to feed. While he could not see all of the village yet what he could see was much larger than any Anishinaabe village he had ever visited. He had been traveling many days and was glad when he thought his journey had ended right there for he believed he would find the greatest chief of all the First Nations people living in such a great village.

As they walked through the cornfields, Turtle told Anung the story of First Corn Plant.

"Corn was proud to be the tallest of the Three Sisters. She was slender but she was strong. The people planted her in the best part of the garden. Corn was happy to look out at the beauty around her. Watching the sunrise and the sun set made her happy. The rainfall made her happy.

"One day she saw two butterflies flying around her. As the butterflies danced their wings brushed against each other. This made Corn sad for she missed being close to a family. As the butterflies flew off she sang her song of loneliness.

"When the sun rose the next morning Corn saw that Squash Maiden had made her way towards her. Squash Maiden had heard Corn's lonely song and she reached out with her vines and grew close to offer her friendship. Corn said, no Megwetch, we cannot grow together. You may be my Sister, but you wander everywhere while I stand in one place. I grow tall and slender to share the sunlight with my young Corn plants. Your broad leaves will block the sun and my young plants will not grow. You must grow alone.

"Bean heard this and planted herself next to Corn. Her slender vines spread out always reaching for something to lean on. She touched Corn gently and softly wrapped herself around her stalk and leaves. They grew tall together. So they became Sisters and learned they should grow close together this way."

Anung saw how the people of this great village planted the Three Sisters. They planted their beans with their corn, and their squash grew in a separate field. He saw that the plants were stronger and the ears on the corn plants were bigger than those that grew in the gardens of his village. He saw there were many more beans growing all along the vine. He would remember and would tell the people of his village the story of the Three Sisters when he returned.

Beyond the corn field Anung saw one of the sacred herbs had been planted. It was a patch of Asemaa. There were men of this village working in the field, cutting some of the broad green leaves of the Asemaa plants.

These men appeared very different from the men of Anung's village. They wore their hair like the men of his village. But where he could see their skin it was covered with colorful pictures. Some of these were pictures of the animals of the forests. Some were designs. The men of his village did not decorate their bodies like this.

When these men spotted Anung they greeted him warmly and waved for him to come forward. The people of this great village were Odawa, brothers of the Anishinaabe, and they could see Anung was Anishinaabe.

Anung did not need Turtle to understand and speak with these men for they shared many words.

Anung told the Odawa men of the vision that drove his journey. He told them he had been traveling many days off the paths and trails of his people for he was looking for the greatest chief of all the First Nations people.

He told the men that to keep his journey on the true direction he had walked through the thickest forests. He had climbed over many dead falls. He had to break through thickets of branches and vines. He swam lakes and rivers.

And he always kept his eyes and ears opened for Windigo.

The men told Anung he was brave to journey through the forests alone. They told him their chief was not the greatest chief of all the people, for some men of their village had visited a greater chief who lived to the East in the land their ancestors lived when they were one people, before they became the Brothers of the Three Fires. But the chief of their village was a good man and he would be honored to meet such a brave boy.

They took Anung to meet their chief. His name was Trout. Anung told Trout of his vision. He showed Trout the stick that bore a notch for each day he had traveled and the stick was covered on all sides. He had begun his journey during the last days of Niibin. Now Dagwaagin was soon to give way to the cold winds and snow of Biboon.

Trout told Anung that living in his village were men who traveled the forests and the waters farther than any other people for the Odawa were the greatest traders of all the First Nations people.

Once the men of this village traveled along The Great River that flowed to the East.

They followed the river to a great salt lake so big the water stretched the sky and the lake and the sky met as far as the eye could see. On the shore of this salt lake the men found a village much larger than any they had seen in their travels. The Odawa traders spoke of the great herds of caribou they found to the North. He told Anung that in this great village his men said there were as many people as there were caribou in the greatest herd.

Their Three Sisters gardens grew all around this great village, and each garden was bigger than the Odawa village.

Each net they used to fish the great salt lake that stretched the sky was longer than all of the Odawa's nets sewn together.

They carved great canoes from the biggest trunks of the tallest trees.

They had walls made of tall tree trunks all around their village.

Their wigwams within the walls were as long as the course the boys mark when they run their races.

They had storehouses with furs of beaver and mink piled higher than a man could reach.

There were visitors from many tribes in this great village. The Odawa traded with many tribes but at this great village they met men from places they had never visited or even heard stories of before. Many strange languages were heard. Many strange customs of dress were seen.

Trout told Anung that the chief of this village was the greatest chief of all the First Nations people. And that the journey to this village would take so many days that Anung must find himself a new stick to mark the days to come.

All these things Trout told Anung.

That night Anung beat his father's drum and sang the song that had come with him on his journey. It was the song of his village.

He sang of when he was a boy and how one man made him snowshoes so Anung had a good pair when he was with the men checking their traps. He sang how another taught him how to make snowshoes for himself as a man.

Anung sang about the women of his village who cared for him when he was sick. How each woman of his village always prepared a serving of food for him and only gave it to their children when they knew Anung had been fed at another fire.

All night the Odawa village had a feast for Anung. They cooked their best meats. They sang their most joyful songs to Gitche Manitou. They thanked the Great Spirit for leading Anung to their village. They gave him a song of the Odawa trading routes to take with him on his journey, and they asked the spirits of their ancestors still roaming these forests to guide and protect Anung on his way.

The young men and women danced for many hours around many fires. All the Nokomis danced around the Grandmother fire while the elders beat the drums.

They gave a large leaf of Asemaa to Anung. This was so he might remember to thank Gitche Manitou during his journey. They burned much of the Asemaa they harvested in the fire as their offering and the smoke carried their prayers for Anung's safe journey to the heavens. They smoked the rest of the Asemaa in their best pipes that they shared with each other.

They filled Anung's pouch with pemmican and dried meats. They gave him all the good breads he could carry.

Each man of the village came to Anung to tell what he knew about the forests and the waters ahead. There was a treacherous ridgeline with a narrow passage and they told Anung how to navigate it. Then he would pass through the lands of the Wyandotte. They warned Anung that he may not be greeted so warmly there. For the Wyandotte were not brothers of the Odawa or Anishinaabe or Pottawattamie. Some villages act as if they are. But some villages do not.

The next morning when Anung awakened in the Odawa village there was the first freezing touch of Gashkadino-Giizi. Before the sun rose, the work of the people of this Odawa village was to rebuild their fires to feel the warmth and prepare to cook the first meal.

Geese flew over Anung's head. The aspen leaves were putting on their gold. The cold Keewatin winds would soon surround them.

The Odawa fed Anung. Then they gave him one of their finest possessions, a coat that would keep him warm when the snows fell. It was made from a white buck deerskin. Inside the coat was a full beaver vest.

When Odawa traders traveled to the West where the prairies touched their forests they found Dakota who brought buffalo robes to trade with them. They gave Anung their finest buffalo robe.

Anung was happy to receive these gifts. He put on the coat. He wrapped the buffalo robe in a bundle and carried it on his back. He walked into the forests towards the land of the rising sun.

WINTER APPROACHES

AT FIRST THE COLD MORNINGS became warm days but soon Anung felt the cold deep into the day. The stone from his sling flew behind the grouse. And he caught only the smallest ground squirrels in his snares. So he was glad to have been given such good food by the Odawa.

But after days passed and the night's bitter cold held tight to the day, the food he had been given was gone.

Now the stone from his sling was deflected away by the branch of a tree. Now his snares were empty. Before he could get close enough to a deer for a killing shot with his bow, the deer heard him and vanished in the forest.

Four days passed when Anung had no food but a few dried berries. He was growing very hungry and very weak. That was when he spied Squirrel sitting on a branch scratching his ear with his hind foot. Squirrel nodded to Anung then turned and disappeared into his hole in the tree. Anung climbed the tree to try to catch Squirrel in his tree hole. When he looked inside the hole he saw Squirrel sitting next to a great pile of nuts. Squirrel was scratching his side with his hind foot. Anung could feel the hunger pains in his stomach growing sharper.

Anung removed Turtle from his pouch so Turtle could tell Squirrel of Anung's deep fierce hunger. Squirrel scratched his belly then offered to share his nuts with Anung and Turtle. Anung was so weak he could not crack open the nuts so Squirrel cracked them open with his teeth and gave the best parts to Anung and Turtle to eat.

After they had been well fed Anung repaid Squirrel by playing his father's drum for him and singing the songs of his journey to find the greatest chief.

Then it was time to sleep. Squirrel scratched his chest with his hind leg. He chewed the base of his tail with his teeth. He scratched so much that Anung could not sleep lying next to Squirrel so he moved away to the far side of the hole.

In the morning Squirrel gave Anung some nuts to take on his journey.

As the sun rose to fill the forest, Anung began scratching his arms and his legs. Something was burning his skin and making it itch. He did not know what it was. As he walked on, first he scratched behind his ear, then under his arm, then he scratched his scalp, and with every step he scratched and scratched.

First Anung could smell the smoke and then, ahead, rising above the trees, still at some distance, Anung could see smoke. He scratched his neck and his stomach and walked in the direction of the smoke, hoping to find a village. As he drew closer he could hear strange voices. It seemed there were many voices singing many different songs but he could not understand the songs for he could not understand their words.

On the trails leading through the forest towards where the smoke rose, Anung saw people walking together. Then he could see they were carrying many bundles. When he came closer he was surprised to see what was wrapped in the bundles for each one carried the body of a dead family member. Some had been dead for a long time. He could see some had recently died.

Turtle told Anung this was a village of Wyandot and that they speak a different language. Then he explained to Anung that some Wyandot bury their dead first in the ground near the dead person's favorite place so their spirit can say goodbye to that place. And some Wyandot build small shelters for their dead on the tops of scaffolds that sit along a path the dead one's family will follow, so the family can say goodbye to the spirit.

Then every ten years the Wyandot collect all these dead parents and children and return with them to their village. The songs they were singing as they passed by were the songs the living sang to the spirits of their dead.

Anung came out of the forest to the widest path to the village. Many on this path were carrying bundles. Others carried the pots or the war clubs or the medicine bags or the blankets that had been left with their family members to use in the next world.

When the men of this village saw how Anung was scratching himself they stopped him from entering their village with them. Then they called for the elders.

Turtle told Anung that the Wyandot asked him why he was scratching himself like Squirrel. Anung told of being fed by Squirrel, and of sleeping with Squirrel in his tree to stay warm.

The elders told him he must take off all of his clothes. They threw the buckskin coat with the warm beaver vest on a fire and burned it. They burned the buffalo robe next.

One of the elders told the young men to bring water so Anung could bathe. They told him that the squirrels in these trees were stricken with fleas. Some of their people were bitten by these fleas and became very sick, and some of them died and were among the dead present.

After he bathed they gave Anung some clothes to wear. Then they invited him to come into their village for the Feast for the Dead.

All day the Wyandot villagers told stories about their deceased family members and Turtle translated for Anung. And they sang songs to their spirits. They lit many fires to warm the spirits as they gathered to listen to their brothers or wives sing of their lives.

They all sat together on the ground, the living and the dead.

They sang songs for the spirits of their children who died too soon.

They sang songs for their wives who died during a terribly harsh winter and for husbands who left wives all alone in old age, and for brothers and fathers who were killed in a battle for hunting grounds.

They sat on the ground together and sang these songs while they washed the bodies they had gathered. Then they wrapped each body in clean furs and hides.

Anung watched as one Wyandot took the arm of his dead brother and wrapped it with the body of his brother's first daughter and sang of her beauty to him and told her that her father's strength would always protect her.

Another man mixed the bones of his father with his father's trusted hunting companion and sang of their great moose hunts in this world and of the hunts they will enjoy in the next world.

Anung beat his father's drum and sang of his village to the people around him. When Turtle translated for them, the Wyandot told him they would remember his song and would forever consider the Anishinaabe to be their brothers.

Then it was time for the Wyandot to leave their village with their beloved dead, and with the tools and blankets and other treasures their souls would need in the next world.

Turtle explained to Anung that the Wyandot would travel to the Land of the Night. This is where Wyandot from all of the villages gather once every ten years to bury their dead villagers in a common burial ceremony. Together they prepare them for their journey along the Path of Souls. Turtle told him that the Wyandot believe that this unity in the next world creates harmony in this one. It is hard to fight with someone whose mother is buried alongside your own.

The Wyandot left Anung alone in the village as they traveled to the West of Ninggabi' anong. When they were gone Anung left the village on his true path East to find the greatest chief and tell him of all the wonderful creations of the Great Spirit he had found on his journey.

THE FIRST SNOW ARRIVES

EVERY MORNING ANUNG headed East to the first sun. It was getting colder every day and now Turtle was asleep for the winter, wrapped in a fox fur nestled in the bottom of Anung's pouch.

The first snow dusted the ground. Anung was sad he did not have the coat with the full beaver vest and the buffalo robe. He had very little food left, and he was finding less and less each day. His hunger was growing again.

He traveled through forests thick with branches and brush. When the snow fell so hard he could not see, he found a place protected from the worst of the wind and waited so he would not lose his course. When the snow stopped he put on his snowshoes to walk over the drifts that were half as tall as he.

To stay his true course he crawled through a thicket of thorn bushes he could not see his way around. The thicket was so deep it took him two days to crawl through it and he had to make a bed in the middle of it where he slept very little.

The thorns tore his skin in many places. When he finally crawled out he built a fire and did not travel for two days so he could rest and his wounds would heal. He rubbed Bashkodejibik and Giizhikaandagoons to clean his wounds. The Wyandot had given him this sage and cedar for healing.

The snow fell hard while Anung rested.

As the sun was going down the second day, a shadow shape walked between the trees through the windblown snow. It was approaching the clearing where Anung was sitting next to his fire. This shape was big. Not tall enough to be Windigo, but very big. Anung wondered who this man might be.

He saw it was not a man. It was Old Makwa, the black bear, and he was looking for a dry cave for his long winter sleep for it was Biboon's time now. Makwa disappeared into the forests ahead.

Anung slept huddled at his fire. He woke many times to add more wood to keep the flame strong to keep him warm.

The next morning he entered the forests again, headed on his true course East, looking for the greatest chief to tell him of his village.

It snowed every day.

Sun was so ashamed he could not bring more heat to the world and so he came later every morning and left earlier each day. It was always cold and it was dark much of the time. The snow was deep.

Anung had no food. It was hard work staying warm at night. He was tired from his long journey and he was sleeping very little. It was hard work to lift his snowshoes through the heavy snow. He was afraid he was not strong enough to make his path through the snow.

He very cold and he grew weaker all the time.

When all he could think about was the gnawing pain in his stomach and the cold that froze his body, that was the moment Windigo chose to jump from behind a tree to try to snatch up Anung. When Anung saw Windigo coming he turned and gathered all of the energy he had left to run through the snow. Because Windigo was a monster of great size he was slowed by the many trees it had to run around, but because Windigo was as fast as the wind and as powerful as a storm, he could run very fast and he could break through the branches and smaller trees. So Windigo came closer and closer as Anung struggled to run.

Windigo ran so fast the blood splattered from his huge clawed feet and with each step he stained the snow red.

Anung's fear gave him new strength and drove him to run as fast as he could, but Windigo was faster and soon the terrible cannibal was just behind Anung, reaching out his long arms with his massive claws to grab him. Anung could smell his horrible breath and was so afraid.

That is when Anung saw a hole under a ledge at the bottom of a ridge. With his last burst of energy he dove into the hole just as a snow covered branch blocked Windigo's view of Anung's escape and he rushed past, and then howled his anger when he realized he had lost Anung.

Anung found it was dry under the ledge, and the hole led deep into the ground under the ridge. Anung waited until he was sure Windigo had passed, then called down into the hole to tell anyone inside that Anung, an Anishinaabe on a long journey, was coming in and that he promised peace to all he might find. Then he crawled down into the hole.

His body was shivering from the cold so he pulled the pine boughs he had found at the mouth of the hole over on top of him. He had never been so hungry. He had never been so tired. And soon he fell into a deep sleep.

Anung slept a long time.

He had many dreams.

His first dream was of Windigo, chasing him through the snow, coming closer and closer until Anung was snatched away, rescued by his Mother.

In his next dream his Mother had the kind touch of White Cloud, one of the women of Anung's village.

Then he dreamed his Mother had the long soft black hair of Tall Woman, another woman of his village who had cared for Anung.

In another dream his Mother had the warmth of the kind old Nokomis.

In one of his dreams his Mother touched his face. When she did she discovered Anung was hungry and she picked him up and put him to her breast. Anung was very hungry so he drank deeply.

Anung was weak so he drank often.

The milk Anung drank tasted of fully ripened blueberries.

The milk tasted of eggs from the partridge nest. He tasted the freshness of the young trout trapped in the cool headwaters of a stream.

He licked his lips when he tasted the golden sweetness of honey in his Mother's milk.

In his dreams his Mother never left him. She kept Anung sleeping next to her day after day, night after night.

Her body was warm and soft.

Whenever he was hungry she fed him.

He slept to the beat of her heart that soon became the only sound he knew. But then there was another heartbeat and Anung dreamt a child was born. This child wanted his share from his Mother. Anung had never lain next to his Mother so he pushed this baby aside.

His Mother cuffed Anung, then brought him to one breast and the baby to the other and Anung understood this baby was his brother and dreamt they slept side by side in this way for many nights.

In his next dream Anung was traveling through the heavens. There was no land to be seen, just stars all around him. One star was calling out to him but Anung thought this was his home now, here next to his Mother, so he did not answer the call.

In his last dream the long cold winter nights had passed and he was stronger and again he was traveling through the forests with Turtle to find the greatest chief of all the people.

When Anung awoke from his final dream he was not hungry anymore. He was not tired. He felt his strength had returned, and he was ready to continue his journey.

He crawled up to the mouth of the cave. It was dark outside. He sat just inside the mouth of the cave until the sun rose in the East so he could mark his true course.

He stood to look out at the new world of Zigwaan. The snow was melted where Sun was brightest. New green and yellow and purple buds were shooting from branches and soil.

The first birds began to sing.

Then there was a noise from behind him, deep down in the hole. It was coming closer, and Anung could see something moving up from the darkness. He stood aside as Mother Bear crawled from the cave, followed by a newborn cub. As Mother Bear shuffled past, Anung bowed to her and he gave her his thanks.

Mother Bear told him to travel carefully.

The bear cub called Anung Big Brother. Anung called the bear cub Little Brother. Mother Bear led Little Brother into the forest.

Anung pinched some Asemaa from his pouch and sprinkled it at the mouth of the cave as he thanked Gitche Manitou for keeping him safe through the harshest days of the winter.

Then he thanked Memekwesiw, Spirit Boss of the Bears, for feeding him.

THE WATERS THAT STRETCH THE SKY

ANUNG AND TURTLE traveled towards the land of the first sun for many days as Zigwaan's warmth brought the forest back to life.

It became easier to find food now.

He traveled many days next to the Great River the Odawa told of in their stories. It was much wider than the greatest river Anung had ever seen. It was filled with fish in the shallows. He easily speared one for his evening meal.

He found fresh roots and greens everywhere he looked.

Bird nests were filled with eggs. He never took more than one from a nest.

There was a ledge or hollowed tree every night to stay dry and warm.

The sun was big and bright every morning.

After many days of easy travel Anung came upon a path in the forest that followed his course. He followed it for a short time until he came to a clearing where many people were resting. They were each dressed in different styles of clothes, they each had different hair styles and dressings. Turtle told him they were from many different tribes.

After such a long journey Anung wondered if these people were a sign he was near the great village the Odawa had visited, where he would find the greatest chief of all the First Nations people.

Most of these people were speaking in the Iroquois tongue. Some spoke an Algonquian language.

Most of the travelers were men. But there were women as well.

Turtle translated what these people said to Anung.

From the people who gathered there Anung learned that this path led through the forests to a village bigger than any ever seen. It was built on the shore of the great salt lake that stretches the sky. This village was Owasco. All these people were traveling to this village because of the stories being told of the momentous days soon to come when wonderful events would happen there.

Anung joined the people as they gathered their possessions and continued on to the Owasco village.

The people on the path told Anung about the dream this chief had when he was a boy. In his dream he was saw four young men traveling through forests and over tall mountains and across mighty rivers, traveling great distances from their homes, each one alone, each one called to his journey, each coming to this place where the great chief's own dream showed him he was to build this village to prepare for the four young men's arrival.

The first young man had arrived at the great chief's village when the days were still filled with the sun's warmth. That story quickly spread far and wide. The second young man entered the village the same day the winter snows began to fall. The third to arrive came to the village cold and hungry in the middle of a terrible snow storm.

As soon as the snows began to melt, the great chief sent messengers to all of the camps and villages as far as his messengers could travel to tell everyone that two more of the young men from his dream had arrived. Now he was inviting all of the people to come to his village for the celebration that would occur when the forth young man arrived.

After Anung heard these stories he told these people of his dream and of his journey.

He told them of the mothers and fathers of his village who had cared for him and everyone agreed they had taught him well, for he had traveled alone a great distance.

He told these people it was his vision's quest that brought him to this path leading to this village to find the greatest chief of all the First Nations people.

The people who walked with Anung on this path were honored to finish their trip with him for they knew he must be the fourth young man from the great chief's dreams.

Traveling with Anung was an Odawa trader. He had spent many years traveling from village to village and he found there were some stories that all the First Nations people tell. He told one of these stories as they continued along the path through the forests.

"Nanabush was born of a woman. But the father of Nanabush? Ah gee, everyone said his father was Ninggabi' anong, the Spirit of the Western Mountains. It was soon after Nanabush was born this his mother died. Most said her death was an accident. But there were some who said she was killed by Ninggabi' anong and said so when it was safe to say it.

"Nanabush was raised by his grandfather and grandmother. When he asked them about his father and about what had happened with his mother, his grandmother would turn away and say nothing and his grandfather told him he must grow to be a man before he would understand.

"As Nanabush grew to be a young man all the people could see he possessed powers far greater than the other men of his village. That is when they knew he was a man and a spirit. That is when his grandmother told Nanabush that his father had killed his mother and that he was living in the West behind the tallest mountains.

"Nokomis warned Nanabush that though his powers were great among men, his father's powers were far greater. That did not frighten Nanabush. He was a young man who had never tasted defeat at the hands of another in games or battle. He announced to all the people of his village that he would find his father and get revenge for his mother's death.

"He traveled for many moons. When he came to the tallest mountains he grew tired and camped for the night.

"He heard a voice call his name. 'Nanabush', said the voice, 'beware of your father Ninggabi' anong. He knows you are here and he is coming to destroy you with his mighty powers. To protect yourself you must collect flints from the mountains behind you. Collect many pieces. Then sharpen them carefully. Fill up your pouch with all the flints you can find. Tie one sharpened flint around your neck. Flint is the one weapon your father fears.'

"In the tree above him Nanabush saw Woodpecker. It was this bird who had delivered his warning. The next day as the sun rose Nanabush set out to do as Woodpecker directed.

"Nanabush was sharpening the flints he had spent the morning gathering when suddenly his father appeared in his camp. Nanabush had grown big and strong but his father was bigger and stronger.

"They sat on the ground and talked all that day. The sun went down and still they talked. The moon rose and fell and they sat there in that place and talked. Only as the night was ending did Nanabush tell his father he had come to avenge his mother's death.

"To hear his son speak these words made his father sad. He said to his son, 'Yes, my son, I am glad to see you have grown to be such a strong man. I can see that. But I am stronger than you. You can see that. You may be able to hurt me, but you cannot defeat me. You must know there is nothing you can do that will restore your mother's life.'

"Nanabush got up from the ground at this place by the mountains and told his father what he said was true, but he would fight him at this place the next day.

"The next morning they met for battle. Ninggabi' anong shot his arrows at Nanabush so fast the next one was cocked at his bow while the first was still flying through the air. Nanabush threw his flints so hard at his father that the wind changed its course.

"They fought all day in this fashion. At the end of the day all the arrows had been shot and were splintered and all the flints had been thrown and were broken. There was no advantage.

"In the dark they found each other and wrestled on the ground where they sat together and talked the day before. First Nanabush was winning. Then his father was getting the best of Nanabush.

"When it appeared the father would defeat the son, that is when Nanabush removed the flint from around his neck and cut Ninggabi' anong on his head. Ninggabi' anong roared in pain and his hold on his son weakened. He stopped fighting.

"Ninggabi' anong said to his son, 'You are as strong as I am. I cannot defeat you. And you cannot defeat me. This means there must be peace between us. I will live here in my mountains. You return to your village and teach all the people the right ways to live in their lands. In this way you will know the love your mother never gave to you.'

"Then his father gave Nanabush a beautiful bone pipe, carved from an antler, inscribed with all of his wisdoms. He told Nanabush to carry this pipe with him back to his people. It was to be his symbol of peace. He must teach the people of all the villages and clans to bring the ceremonies of the peace pipe to all of their gatherings."

As the story ended Anung could see faint smoke in the distance. The path led to the place where the smoke was rising above the trees. The path led through the forest that began to thin out half way up a long gentle slope of a hill.

As he neared the top of the hill Anung heard a sound he had never heard before. It was a sound made of every sound he had ever heard. It frightened him but it excited him as well.

When he crested the hill this sound grew so large and loud that it filled the sky and echoed back down on him and it stopped Anung in his tracks. Then he saw all at once the most wonderful sights he had ever seen and all of it was so suddenly amazing that he had to sit down hard, right there on the hilltop.

He placed Turtle on the ground next to him and then forgot him for he did not know how to look at so many things at once and he was confused by the sight of it all so he did not stand again for a long time. There was so much to see Anung sat there planted in the ground like a bush for most of the rest of the day. Many travelers passed by on the path that led down the hill across the broad plain on to the village and they wondered who he was as he sat still and quiet and studied all there was laid out before him.

The village, and behind the village, was the great salt lake that stretched the sky. The sounds Anung had heard were coming from the waves on the shore of this great body of water and from the countless number of people constantly working and playing and talking and shouting in and around the village.

The water that went on forever and ever was so vast it first brought fear to Anung's heart. And then confusion, for he had not known his eyes could see so far as this distant horizon. He had always been able to see land on the other side of any lake. But as he sat there and watched the waves begin as a far off swell and then come rolling in one after the other to curl and crest white before they crashed on the shore, he saw in it the beauty of the Great Creator and that comforted him.

After Anung studied the water that stretched the sky, he turned back to look at the village. He had never seen so much activity of life as was happening there. Everywhere there were people, many people, doing everything Anung had ever seen done before, and everywhere there were many people doing so many things he had never seen done before.

It was stunning to see so much at one time.

To imagine the splendor of this great village we are wise to begin to see it instead as an ancient city.

There were more longhouses than Anung could count. Each longhouse was the length of the race he would run against the boys of his village to see who was the fastest among them. Each longhouse was nearly as tall as two men standing on top of each other. And each longhouse had at least two and some had as many as four smoke holes and as Anung watched more smoke rose from more and more holes.

People exited from a longhouse and disappeared into another, they gathered in smalls groups in the open spaces to talk, they tended the cooking fires that grew in number, they shouted greetings and welcomed each new band of arrivals, and they all seemed to take on more activity as the day went on.

Anung was delighted to see how many different tribes were gathered here. He recognized many from the Three Fires, the Anishinaabe, Pottawattamie, and Odawa. The Wyandot were familiar now. But there were many varieties of hair dressings and many different clothing styles that he had never seen.

The city was surrounded three times.

Like a great chief, this city wore a collar, a necklace, and a breastplate.

The collar was the wall of tree trunk posts that surrounded the village. Each post was as tall as two men and was sharpened at the top to a point.

The great village's necklace was made from the dwelling and shelters just outside the walls built by the travelers from nearby villages or far away tribes. So many people had come from other tribes there was no room for all these dwellings inside the city walls, so they had clustered in their own little villages of fully built domed wigwams or tall teepees or quickly assembled shelters covered with bark, or grass mats, or hides from moose or deer or buffalo. These were so numerous they fully surrounded the city walls and more were being constructed.

The city's breastplate was the collection of large and many newly planted gardens. There were rows and rows of established gardens. New gardens were being carved out of the fields. The black earth was dotted with fresh green sprouts of the Three Sisters and of Asemaa and every other kind of plant.

The city and its villages and its gardens covered most of the broad flat plain that led to the beach.

The beach was white sand washed by the great waters. A team of men were pulling a canoe across the beach to the water. This canoe was made from a massive tree trunk and was as large as four canoes from Anung's village. While Anung watched many men launched the canoe through the waves but only one man stayed on board. He paddled for a moment and then raised a post in the middle of the canoe, and the post had a hide attached and Anung watched as it caught the wind that pushed the canoe along. This was just one more strange wonder for Anung.

Off a rocky point men in smaller canoes were pulling in their nets filled with fish. If so many people could be in one place Anung wondered at the number of fish living in this great salt lake.

Some children chased birds on the beach. Some children chased other children as dogs ran at their sides. Anung could not hear the laughter of the children, nor the barking of the dogs for they were lost in the greater sounds, but he could feel their joy.

Then, as he looked back at the life of the city unfolding, he saw how much of it shared in this joy.

When the travelers who had left Anung on the ridge top continued on to the city they sent word to the great chief that the fourth young man had arrived.

The chief declared the celebration would begin after sundown and the word quickly spread as preparation of a great feast became the task of all gathered.

Anung sat at the crest of the hill and watched as the people attended to their duties and more travelers passed by and headed down the hill to the city preparing for the long prophesied moment.

He could see people emerging from their shelters in full headdresses of feathers, and others with red cloth turbans, and animal head caps; women with hair long and flowing free and others with braids; there were heads shaved bald and clean and others shaved bald and painted and some men wore their hair long on their shoulders and some wore their hair straight up like porcupine quills.

He could see some of the people were painting the new hides they'd attached over the doors of their just built shelters and others tied clusters of feathers above the door.

Some of the people were painting themselves, or one another. Some just painted faces. Some men painted their chests and their arms.

They wore loin clothes and leggings, shirts and skirts and dresses, vests and knee high moccasins and they were all decorated with beads and shells and bits of quills and single feathers and feathered arrays.

If they carried weapons they were ceremonial. They were more likely carrying the peace pipe of their village, or a pouch with their magic.

Longhouses were arrayed to present an open space in the center of the city and that is where young men were stacking branches for a large fire as, one by one, old men in full ceremonial dress arrived at this fire circle.

Some of these old men began to beat their drums, big drums, small drums. Some used a beating stick to play their drums. Some used their hands. Other men had rattles.

More cook fires were started inside and outside the village walls as the women were forming work groups. Some women were baking corn breads and others were making fry breads. Some women were roasting venison and moose. Other women were stirring stews of fish and tubers, and soups of fish and leeks, or boiling greens.

Outside the village Anung watched the growing collection of young men, in their warrior dress, taking turns shooting arrows at a tree's target. When one fellow hit the center Anung watched him dance.

Anung felt the wind shift, blowing now from across the water, and over the city, and it bathed him full in his face with new sensations.

Now he could hear the children's laughter.

He tasted salt in the air from the great salt lake that stretches the sky.

The savory smells from the cook fires invited his full hunger.

Anung was sure his journey's end was here. When he looked out over the water he could see there was no place else to go.

His dream had taken him on a journey to the edge of Turtle Island.

When the travelers first spoke of the chief of this city Anung thought he must be the greatest of all the chiefs. After beholding the splendor, he was sure of it.

He was happy to think his quest was ended. He would find this great chief and sing of his village, of his fathers and mothers, and of the wonders he had seen during his journey.

Then he would return to his village. He was eager to return, for he missed his mothers and his fathers. He had much to tell them, new wisdoms and new stories.

He stood and saw Turtle was there waiting for him, so he picked him up and they followed a family down the hill to the great city. When the lookout saw the fourth young man coming down the hill he sent the message to the great chief.

ANUNG SINGS FOR THE PEOPLE OF THE CITY

THE GREAT CHIEF WAS STANDING outside the city's main gate when Anung approached. Behind him stood the three young men the great chief had dreamed would come to this place in search of the great chief. They were eager for their fourth brother to arrive.

Like Anung, they had recently been boys, and they did not hide their eagerness to discover what came next.

The elders of the city were gathering and the chiefs and elders from the many tribes from the many villages who had traveled from near and far to be there stood with them, gathering all around, all the people in their tribal dress.

The great chief stood tall among them. He was dressed plainly, in a long buckskin tunic shirt and leggings. The front half of his head was shaved and he wore a small cluster of feathers in his hair that grew long in the back. He placed his hand on Anung's shoulder and welcomed him and then Turtle. He turned to all those gathered and told them to take care of this weary young man.

Turtle helped Anung understand all those who welcomed him, and the directions of all who would serve him. He was led to his place in the chief's longhouse where he was given a beautiful buckskin vest to wear, the fringes decorated with cowry shells.

They led him to the chief's cook fire where he was given the best portion of roasted venison.

After he ate they followed him as he wandered through the darkening city to explore in the last of the daylight the great salt lake that stretches the sky. He tasted the salt water and spit it out and he laughed at himself when he was surprised it was salty.

As it grew dark the white-capped waves grew even more lovely and Anung was happy to have made this long journey.

They returned when the drums called them to the great fire circle built inside the village walls and they joined all who had gathered there.

Many people were gathered around the fire. Ring after ring after ring of people from all the First Nations were gathered there and many of them had been chanting songs of their tribes and the voices of all the people were heard.

Soon the drums turned the many voices into one song of praise for Gitche Manitou. After they sang four cycles of this song of praise the great chief stood among the people to tell of his dreams.

These dreams first found him before this city had been built.

These dreams first came to him when he was a boy on his own vision quest.

The village he lived in when he had his dream was near the river to the South. This place where now he stood was where his people would camp while they set their nets off the rocky point, for the waters there were always filled with fish, in every season.

In his first dream he saw that four boys would each leave their villages from far away to come to this place where now they were gathered together. The four boys would come to this place from far away in search of the greatest chief of all the First Nations people. His first dream told him that he must greet them when they arrived to warn them that the most difficult, the most dangerous part of journey was still to come.

The four young men looked at each other in surprise, for they all believed their journeys had ended here.

In his second dream this great chief was told to build a city of great acclaim on this site, far greater than any village, and in this dream he saw row after row of longhouses surrounded by a tall wall and abundant gardens.

The third dream showed him that he was to build this great city to attract many wise elders who would come to this place to see it and then stay to live together to learn from each other. And many brave men would come, the greatest warriors and hunters, and stay to learn from each other and to study the powers found in the wise men's words. This great city would become a home to Nokomis from the villages all around who know the ancient wisdoms and to strong women who would teach the men what only women know. These great leaders of their people would build the best tools. They would use these tools to make the finest crafts. And they would know how to prepare all the food a man would need for many days of travel.

His fourth dream told him that the journey for three of these young men would end here. But the fourth young man must continue across the great salt lake that stretches the sky. He must find his way across the first water, the remains of the flood waters that once covered the earth and that still surround Turtle Island. For the great chief's dream told him that the old legends were true, that there was another island across the water, a much bigger island, the island of the first sun.

The great chief understood that his city must be built to prepare one of these young men for his journey across the flood waters to find the island of the first sun. For his dream told him that is where the greatest chief will be found. And one of these young men must continue his journey to find the greatest chief to tell him the stories and sing the songs of all of the people of Turtle Island.

And this young man will then return to his people, with the wisdom he learned from the greatest chief.

His dreams showed him how men of this village would make great canoes out of the biggest trees. The men of this village have paddled those canoes on a course to the island of the first sun many times. They have taken many trips to locate this faraway place so they might tell the chosen one who will continue his journey what they find.

Some of these men paddled their canoes until they could not be seen by their wives or children.

Some never came back.

Others returned after many days without ever finding the land they were searching for.

Many were too afraid to venture any further when they got to the point they could barely see shore. They returned.

In his dreams the great chief saw how the best craftsmen and women would work together to stitch the finest buck skins together and mount them across a great stick frame that resembled in many ways the frame of a giant's snowshoe. The dreams showed how this hide could catch the winds and capture their power to push the canoe along the waves faster than many men could paddle.

The men of this village built this sail and ventured far across the great water, but they still did not find any land.

They decided that only the chosen one would find it.

His last dream told him that as the great chief it was he would decide which young man would travel on to find the greatest chief.

The chief asked the elders of all the tribes gathered there to tell him how they would select the young man who would continue on. After much discussion they agreed that each young man must sing the song he would sing when he stands before the greatest chief. The elders and chief would then watch the people as each song was sung, and the people's response would tell them who was to be the chosen one.

Anung sat near the fire with the young men.

He was afraid to sing his song in front of so many people.

When he first stood at the shore of the great salt lake that stretches the sky he was struck silent. Now, being there before all the people gathered around the fire, he felt like he did when standing in front of those waves for the first time. He was afraid that when it was his turn to sing his song that this tightness in his throat would only get tighter and he would not be able to make a sound.

The young man who arrived at the village first stood to sing first. He was Wabanaki. He had the shortest distance to travel and had arrived during the warm summer days. His head was shaved but for a knot on top that was decorated with feathers. He had painted a thick red stripe above his eyes and a thin black stripe below them, and wore a quill breastplate.

He sang a Wabanaki song. His song told of the days he had traveled over rivers and lakes. His song told of his arrival at the village. He sang about what he learned by studying the great waters, for it had revealed many of its secrets to him. In his song he told of building his own canoe to travel far out on the great salt lake that stretches the sky.

The people had seen this Wabanaki out in his canoe, even in the fiercest storms. They nodded as he sang his song and told each other it was a good song to sing.

The young man who arrived during the snowstorm rose to sing next. His hair was long and rested on his shoulders that were covered by his buckskin shirt. He wore no paint, and just one feather hung down from the back of his head.

He sang a Natchez song. He sang of the wisdom his people gained living in the rhythms of the Father River that floods Turtle Island every Spring but always returns to its course, leaving the land it had just covered with water now rich with the best soil it carried down from the North. He sang of his travel to the rising sun where he found the shore of the first waters far to the south of this great Owasco city.

He sang of the days he walked the shore and his song asked the spirits of the wind why one day the waves gently licked the shore and the next day they crashed in a great white-headed fury.

And he sang of the way the people cared for him arriving at the Owasco village in the middle of a great snowstorm.

The people remembered the furious winds and blinding snow the day this young man who looked a boy stumbled into their village and they told each other he was brave.

The third young man who arrived just as the snows started to fall stood to sing next. He had journeyed from the Blue Misted Mountains. He began his song in Cherokee. Much of his head was shaved as well but the hair left grew into a long tail down his neck. The top half of his face was painted red. On his bare chest rested a necklace of bear claws.

He sang of the great nation of clans and tribes his people built along the rivers that course through the Blue Misted Mountains. There were many rivers, filled with fish, and many villages with many great chiefs. Some of their villages were nearly as large as this one. Their shelters were not so large as the longhouses, but there were many of them, built with logs, and there were great council houses where the people gathered to advise the chiefs.

He sang of a great nation where the peace chiefs were as powerful as the war chiefs.

Then this young man brought surprised smiles from the people when he sang in the language of the Odawa as he told of the many villages he passed during his journey to this place.

Then he finished his song in Owasco, the father of all Iroquois languages, and sang of the greatness of this city where he had met so many wise elders, where he had seen so many wonders and delights, and that he knew as soon as he met the chief of this village that he was the greatest chief of all the people.

The people turned to the great chief and nodded their approval.

Then it came time for Anung to sing his song.

But he could not sing. The joy he felt in hearing the others sing left him and his throat was tightening again. He could not even stand for his legs were weak.

The elder sitting next to Anung picked up his drum and handed it to him, and nodded to him, that he should play it for them. Anung stayed sitting, set his father's drum in place, and with his beater stick he struck his drum so softly only those close to him could hear it. Then he felt the heartbeat of his Mother from his winter dream and he followed that beat, and when that beat was steady it grew louder and when it was true he began to sing his song.

He sang of the people of his village. To the beat of his Mother's love filled heart he sang of all of his mothers who never let their children eat the last portion of a meal until they knew Anung had been fed. He beat the drum a little faster as he sang of all his fathers of his village who taught him how to honor the spirit of the deer he killed with his arrow. And who showed him how to respect Nokomis.

He beat the drum slowly again when he sang of how tired and hungry he had been when the winter's cold and snow were more than he could survive, then a faster drum beat accompanied the song of Windigo chasing him through the snow and of his narrow escape and of his long winter nap with Mother Bear who nursed him until he regained his strength to continue his journey.

He ended his song as a lament, confessing his fear of traveling alone over the great salt lake that stretches the sky to an island no one has seen. He sang as he told them he has felt this loneliness many times before, whenever he was sad that he never knew his mother or his father.

The people of the city answered with their own soft crying songs, for as Anung finished singing he continued to drum and other men began to drum with him.

Some of the gathered people began dancing to the beat of many drums. The truth of Anung's song was still heard in the drums and the people dancing made spirits shout.

As more of the people got up to dance, the great chief placed his hand on Anung's shoulder and said here was the chosen one. The people sang his name and asked him to tell them more of his journey. As he told them his story many of the people came up to him to give him their gifts.

ANUNG CROSSES
THE FIRST WATERS

THE NEXT MORNING the city prepared Anung's canoe for him. The craftsmen of this Owasco city had learned the best way to manage the slowest burn to hollow out a great tree trunk to make the largest canoe with sides so light and strong the canoe could handle the roughest weather.

Each of the tribes gathered at the great city smoked or dried their meats and fish and they prepared their best for Anung. Along with breads and squash and corn they collected enough food for Anung to last a long journey to the island of the first sun. The lightest and strongest baskets using the best methods and materials of the gathered people were woven to store the food.

The best bladders of hides were used to store water, for skins were much lighter than even the finest clay pots.

They loaded Anung's canoe with as much food and water as the canoe would hold.

The canoe was narrow, to cut through the waves cleanly. An outrigger was mounted on its side to keep it stable. They studied the construction of the best snowshoes and the most flexible and durable lacrosse sticks to build the framework for the canoe's sail, then sewed a sail of the finest buckskin that was scrapped many times to make it the lightest buckskin they had ever made.

A great red sun was painted on the sail, but there was still room for all of the symbols of the gathered tribes. Each took their turn and decorated the sail with signs and images so every tribe would be known to the greatest chief when Anung found him across the great salt lake that stretches the sky.

When Turtle learned that Anung's journey would take them to a distant island he did not want to leave Turtle Island so he decided to stay. His gift for Anung was to teach him the chant that would call on the Great Sea Turtle to bring him help should he need it, and then they said goodbye.

All the people of the city and all of the travelers gathered on the beach as a procession of singers led the warriors chosen to launch Anung's canoe from the beach and out into the water, pushing it past the waves. They had been singing songs of this Anishinaabe boy and of his people in his village as they walked across the sands with him. As he headed off shore they sang to him that he was now the son of each of the tribes and of the brother of all of the people.

Anung liked this song, and he sang it as he shot down the back side of the waves. When the wind caught the sail he was excited to feel the power. He set the tiller to sail to the East, and for this moment he forgot he was afraid.

When the sail caught the first wind and the canoe leapt forward over the waves like a deer jumping over a brush pile the people stopped singing. They stood together and watched silently all day until the canoe and then the great red sun painted on the sail disappeared in the dusk where the new sun would rise the next morning. Then they went back to the city and continued their celebration.

The winds filled Anung's sail and pushed him along his true course, to the East and the island of the greatest chief of all the people. He looked back to see how quickly these winds were driving him away from Turtle Island and when the people became so small he could only see them as small dark shapes on a beach his fear of being all alone out on this great body of water returned. He studied the many symbols and images that had been painted on the sail and that comforted him.

When the elders showed Anung how to control the sail they told him to take it down at night so shifting night winds would not blow him off course while he slept. As it grew dark the first night he released the bindings that held the sail in place. He draped the hide over the rigging and folded it into a shelter, and sat under it to rest.

He looked up at the stars. Far off he heard a splash, and then another, and later another, but all else was quiet. He played the drum softly so he wouldn't disturb the silence, just calling to those spirits of the night close to him, asking them to comfort him, and he fell asleep dreaming of his village.

For many days the winds carried Anung's canoe to the East. His sailing was fast so he traveled far. The elders showed him how trailing a long rope behind the canoe will help him keep his bearings. Once he was on the true course, all he had to do was steer the canoe so the rope behind him was always straight.

When another great distance was passed he would lean forward in the canoe to search the far horizons for land but saw none in any direction, and that would bring back his fear. But the winds continued, day after day, and because he had traveled great distances he hoped to find the island soon.

Then one morning as he raised his sail he found the winds had shifted so he lowered it again for it would have taken him off his course. Anung picked up his paddle and continued on his way to the island of the first sun. He paddled all that day, checking that the rope was always straight. Because he worked so hard that day he drank much more water and ate much more food than he had the days the winds had powered him along.

That night when he folded the sail for his shelter he was too tired to play the drum and he fell fast asleep.

The next day the winds did not blow at all and he had to paddle his course for the whole day. He was more frightened than ever, to be all alone in the middle of this great water, and now he was afraid that if the winds didn't return he would run out of food and water before he found the island of the first sun.

Before he slept he played the drum and called on the spirits of Ninggabi' anong to send his wind. For many days after that the West winds came and again he traveled great distances on his true course, his rope straight.

He played the drum every night.

During the first days of travel rain refreshed him, and washed him clean. Then came a time when there were many rain storms day and night. The wind tossed the waters back and forth and the waves crashed over the sides of canoes and he was always wet and cold and some of the food would be destroyed in each storm.

Each time the lightning and thunder approached with the dark clouds gathering, Anung lowered his sail and covered his food and his water with it. Before he tied this bundle to the mast he wrapped his drum in his shirt and tied it to the mast, under the bundle.

When he had to paddle his canoe over waves nearly as tall as the trees of his forest he would tie himself to the canoe as well, for many times the waves nearly washed him away.

After every storm Anung knew to wait until dark for the stars to appear to regain his bearing, to mark East.

The last storm was the biggest. He was paddling across a mountain of a wave when it crashed down on top of him. The rope holding him to the canoe came undone and Anung was thrown from the canoe. As the water rushed over him he was confused and frightened. Then another great wave drove him down deeper and deeper into the water and he remembered the chant Turtle had taught him. He could not say it aloud but in his heart he sang it over and over.

It was dark and Anung was very afraid and when he swam he did not even know for certain if he was swimming to the surface.

Soon Anung's lungs began to ache. But he kept singing the chant in his heart.

It was getting colder and darker and he realized he had not been swimming to the surface but deeper into the water. He was out of breath.

Soon he was so close to death he thought he saw the glimmering lights of the Path of Souls to the next world. That was when the Great Sea Turtle swam into view. Anung grabbed on to the edge of its massive shell and the Great Sea Turtle swam back to the surface with Anung holding tight.

When they surfaced Anung gulped a big breath of air. Then he saw the storm had passed.

THE LAND
OF THE FIRST SUN

ANUNG DID NOT KNOW how long he slept on the Great Sea Turtle's shell, but when he awoke it was a new morning. Anung saw the sun rise over a distant horizon of land.

He rode on the back of the Great Sea Turtle's shell until they got close to shore. Anung slipped from its back and stepped from the waves onto shore.

He gave thanks to the Great Sea Turtle, for with its help Anung's journey had taken him to the land of the first sun. And as Anung rested on the shore and considered what he would do next, the Great Sea Turtle returned, with Anung's canoe balanced across his back.

When it washed to shore Anung discovered his belongings were lost except the small bundle of his shirt tied to the mast. Inside was his father's drum. Anung picked it up and sang a song of thanks to the Great Creator and to the Spirit of Turtle.

He pulled the canoe well up on shore, and when his clothes were dried in the sun he left the beach and headed East.

It was a strange land he discovered. He walked all day under a bright sun for there were very few trees growing at this place and none as beautiful as the trees in the forests that cover Turtle Island.

In many places the earth was as much sand as soil. In other places it was rocky.

There were strange looking birds singing the wrong songs. He was very hungry and the berries he found had the wrong taste. The winds were filled with strange smells.

On the second day Anung saw people gathered together along a hillside. Many were sitting around a cook fire. Those standing held long staffs and watched a flock of crying animals grazing on the sparse grass around them.

He had never seen animals like these on Turtle Island. They looked like milkweed seed pods just beginning to burst.

When he approached these people they looked very different from any of the people he saw during his journey across Turtle Island. They wore long robes with hoods over their heads. The men grew hair on their faces, and on some it was long.

These people had stopped for a meal when Anung found them. When they offered Anung water and food he could not understand the words they spoke but he knew their meaning.

After he ate and drank he sang a song of thanks with the drum's beat.

When he drummed his thanks he also called for any spirits who might be looking for him, to see him in this strange land. The spirits who came to Anung showed him that he should travel with these people, so that is what he did.

When it was night the travelers camped at the edge of a small grove of trees that grew around a spring at the base of a hill. Other bands of travelers were already there and others arrived after them. Some shared their food with Anung. When he played his drum to the spirits that lived in that grove they all drew close to listen to the singing of this young man from far away who appeared no more than a boy to some of them.

The spirits of the grove heard Anung's song and gave all these travelers the gift of understanding each other's words as long as they were under the canopy of its trees. A member of each traveling band told Anung of their destination and its purpose.

Anung told them of his journey from Turtle Island and of the winds and storms that carried him across the great salt lake that stretches the sky. He told him he was looking for the greatest chief of all his people, for when he found him his journey would come to an end and he could return home. When he found him he would sing the song of his village and he would sing a song that would tell this great chief about all the people of Turtle Island.

One of the travelers told Anung that he had once sailed far out into these great waters. He sailed so far that land had vanished. He had heard many tales of the magical land to be found across the waters where Anung had come from, but he had never met anyone who had journeyed across.

Another traveler told Anung that they were also looking for the greatest chief of all their tribes. They travel to him to pay him honor. They had heard that the greatest chief was in a village not so very far off. They would arrive there the next day. They asked Anung if he would travel with them the rest of the way for it seemed they must be searching for the same chief.

They traveled all day. As the sun drew close to rest Anung saw the village, across a great plain, atop a low hill.

They approached the village as night settled around them. Anung saw this village was as strange as the people he was traveling with, for the shelters were all made out of clay like the pots his people made.

As they approached the village a small band of people came from the village and they spoke with great excitement but Anung could no longer understand them. Most of the travelers in Anung's band continued on. Others seemed angry and headed back. Anung followed those who entered the village.

The clay shelters were small. They passed many of them until they came to the far side of the village where the strange animals the villagers kept were in their own clay shelters that were even smaller.

There was a gathering of people there among the animals. Some were quiet. Some were singing songs of praise. Others were dancing to the songs.

Anung followed his new friends to a small room behind the last animal shelter, where the glow of a lantern bathed all in a soft gold.

First Anung saw the mother, shining in the light, sitting in a dry corner. A new born baby was wrapped in cloth and lying in a basket on the ground in front of her. Behind her stood the father, acting like the fathers of Anung's village. The father knew a new baby was the mother's to care for, and it was his job to care for the mother. The time for the father to teach his son would come later.

When the travelers approached them the mother looked at Anung and he felt as if all of his mothers from his village were looking at him with their deepest affection.

The father did not appear to be a chief, nor even a warrior or medicine man. He seemed like all the other men Anung was traveling with, and Anung wondered what made this man the greatest chief. Then he saw those he had been traveling with were laying down their gifts for the baby.

Anung approached the baby in his basket laying at his mother's feet. As he came near he turned his face to the sky above them to see the shimmering lights dancing across the Northern sky.

The lights he saw were the lights he saw in the night sky over his village. When the people of Anung's village saw Wawasayg, the Northern Lights, they knew their ancestors were dancing and singing in the Land of Souls.

That these lights appeared at that moment, just over the baby, told Anung it was this new born child who was the greatest chief of all the people.

It was here at the end of his long journey that Anung hesitated. The others he was traveling with had gifts for this baby. He was afraid he would be dishonoring Gitche Manitou and shaming his village and all the people of Turtle Island because he had no gift to place before this baby, the greatest chief.

The people who had traveled with Anung gestured to his drum, and showed him that he should stand before the baby and play his drum for him, and sing for him. And that is what Anung did.

Under the shimmering lights he played his father's drum for the baby. He played while he sang of the mothers of his village and he sang of the fathers. More of the people danced as Anung sang of all of the wonderful gifts of Gitche Manitou that he had seen and enjoyed during his long journey. He sang about all the people he had met from the many tribes of Turtle Island.

Then Anung asked for the greatest chief's blessing for these people, and for his safe return home.

The mother smiled at him and though he did not understand her, Anung knew she was blessing his voyage. Then the father put his hand on Anung's shoulder and spoke his peace.

All of the travelers found dry places to sleep, and in the morning Anung left his new friends and headed back to the shore where he had left his canoe.

Anung found his canoe and sailed and paddled through many storms to return to Turtle Island.

Once again the Great Sea Turtle came to his rescue.

When he returned to Turtle Island Anung followed a new path through the forests, visiting many new villages along the way. Everywhere he went he told his stories of his great journey and of the baby who was the greatest chief of all the tribes.

He had been gone for many years when he arrived back at his village where he was to live a long and happy life.

EPILOGUE

WHEN MY GRANDFATHER finished telling me this story, I found my grandmother had spread our mat out on the floor and covered it with my favorite foods. There was a pot of venison stew, with manoomin. There was a plate of squash. Next to it was a basket of fry bread. And a big bowl of blueberries mixed in the syrup of the sugar bush.

After we finished our meal, my grandfather planned to walk his trap line. He wouldn't be back until after dark. He had just finished making a new pair of snowshoes for me so I could go with him.

AUTHOR'S NOTE

DEAR STEVE,

When you told me the story of Anung I was immediately captured by the magic of it. When you asked me to popularize it, I was honored by your request. Where I have added to it, your magic has guided me.

I am one of many who owe you thanks. Though we were both just 15 that first summer we met at Delaney Lake, you took care of me like a big brother. You showed me how to do my jobs as a fishing camp laborer, you showed me the best places to fish and how to manage the portages and prepare shore lunch so that I was ready to be a fishing guide, and you showed me the truths and beauties of your family's Ojibway culture. After just one summer with you my life would never be the same, and I was fortunate to have spent four.

You have battled bravely and tirelessly for your people, to the point of exhaustion and beyond. When the day comes that the people of Grassy Narrows can say they have received justice for the Mercury Poisoning that created such devastation, your leadership will be celebrated for its great importance. I hope to be with my Brother when that day comes.

I made a promise to you that night you told me the legend of Anung, after we fished the English River together for the first time in nearly 40 years. That promise is recorded here for the first time.

You asked me to do my best to turn this legend into a full story that would delight and inform people of all ages and all cultures, and I promised you I would. I promised to work to get it published. And I promised that if Anung was published and widely read that, along with accomplishing your goals and fulfilling my promise, I would invest a share of the financial success back into the health of Grassy Narrows.

I look forward to that happening and will work just as hard on the promotion of the book as I did on writing it.

Thanks Steve.

Your Brother,
Carl

THE MUSEUM
OF OJIBWA CULTURE

FIVE YEARS AGO dear friends of mine, Pres and Bess, took me to the Museum of Ojibwa Culture, in St. Ignace Michigan, on the Upper Peninsula shore of the Straights of Mackinac, and I thank them. The Museum's indoor and outdoor exhibits are fully expressive of the cultural history of the Ojibwa, with a focus on the time when the first French voyageurs found the Ojibwa and the Wyandot Huron living gracefully in accordance with the natural laws of the place.

I was captivated, and inspired, by the Museum's portrayal of the many centuries long Ojibwa migration of the Original People moving from the Atlantic Ocean to the Great Lakes and north. The Ojibwa were led West well before the first Europeans arrived by their visions of Megis and just the summer before Steve Fobister had shared with me the legend of Anung, tracing the boy's journey along the same route back East, back to the ancestral home, where he hoped to find the greatest chief.

I introduced myself then to Shirley Sorrell, Director of the Museum and its Cultural Center. I outlined the Anung story for her, and I asked if I could get in touch with her again if the story was ever published. I did, and I was humbled by her offer to host the book's launch at the Museum.

This place, the Straights of Mackinac, is sacred to the book's stories; it's where Mishee Mackinakong, the Great Sea Turtle, rose from the flood waters so Sky Woman could rebuild Turtle Island on the back of his shell. For Anung to be rooted here as it tells the stories it is meant to tell is humbling.

Along with the exhibits and an extensive bookstore, the Cultural Center sponsors a Tribal Youth Entrepreneurship Program, teaching the next generation native and contemporary crafts as well as basic business skills. I was pleased to have the chance to conduct some creativity workshops with the young entrepreneurs.

If you would like to support the Museum and the Cultural Center's programs, you can contact them at museumofojibwaculture. net.

ANUNG ON STAGE

I GRATEFULLY ACKNOWLEDGE indebtedness to poet and playwright Robin Metz for his play, *Anung's First American Christmas* (copyright 2008), based on my draft narrative and a traditional story of the Annishinable (Ojibway) people, as told to me by Steve Fobister. In his play, Robin Metz transforms Turtle (Mishike) into Anung's spiritual guide, and creates Trumpeter Swan, One Antler, Cheengwum, Ningobianong, Crooked Stick, Whale, and many others, gives them voice, and dramatizes a fusion of Native American and Christian beliefs in a vision of rebirth and renewal. The play's central emblem is a towering dream catcher representing space/time, memory, imagination, and the seamless web of life.

I also acknowledge with gratitude Vitalist Theatre's World Premiere production of *Anung's First American Christmas* in a six week run (2008-2009) at Theatre Building Chicago (production and design copyright 2008). The Vitalist Theatre production was directed by Elizabeth Carlin-Metz, who brought her own artistic vision to bear on elements of the play. The production team included set design by Craig Choma; light design by Gina Patterson; costume design by Rachel Sypniewski; sound design by Gregor Mortis; movement, puppetry, and fight direction by Molly Feingold; puppet and mask design by Tracy Otwell; percussion master, W. Carson Hooley; properties master, Kat Powers; projections artists, Brita Nordgren and Tracy Otwell; stage manager, Nicole Smith.

THE MAGIC OF BRITA WOLF

I KNOW IT IN MANY FORMS.

And as I was working on the final drafts of *Anung's Journey* I knew I wanted that illustrative magic of hers to inform your reading of these stories. I wanted her to illustrate this book for you because I had already seen the Turtle Shell you'll find on the cover of this book; she created it for a stage production based on this legend, *Anung's First American Christmas* by the Vitalist Theatre Company in Chicago. The original artwork of the Turtle Shell is 23 inches by 18 inches, and it was framed at the entrance to the theater.

I think the magic found in these images is fully revealed when you learn how they were created—the Turtle Shell and all of the illustrations in the book are reproductions of Brita's paper cuttings. Look at two of my favorites, Eagle Feather and Turtle, and wonder at how this art so gracefully emerges.

I am proud to say that Brita Wolf is my daughter, and I have seen her magic delight many before. I am so happy that her gift is shared here with you.

THE AUTHOR

CARL NORDGREN WAS BORN in Greenville, Mississippi where his great grandmother's house was across the street from the boyhood home of author Walker Percy. Carl has worked as a fishing guide on the English River in Northwestern Ontario and on the White River in the Arkansas Ozarks, as a bartender, a foundry man, and an entrepreneur. He currently teaches courses in Creativity to undergraduate students at Duke University. Carl graduated from Knox College and lives in Durham, North Carolina with his wife Marie where they have raised three daughters. His first novel, *The 53rd Parallel*, spans mid-century Ireland and Canada, weaving a tale about the power of dreams, the hope of new beginnings, and the dangers of ghosts who haunt our past. It is the first in a triology.